The Berenstain Bears
and the PRIZE PUMPKIN

1st Prize, 2nd Prize,
3rd Prize or none—
At Thanksgiving time,
more than a contest
is won.

A First Time Book®

The Berenstain Bears
and the
PRIZE PUMPKIN

Stan & Jan Berenstain

Random House 🏠 New York

Copyright © 1990 by Berenstains, Inc. All rights reserved under
International and Pan-American Copyright Conventions. Published in
the United States by Random House, Inc., New York, and simultaneously
in Canada by Random House of Canada Limited, Toronto.

Library of Congress Cataloging-in-Publication Data:
Berenstain, Stan. The Berenstain Bears and the prize pumpkin /
Stan & Jan Berenstain.   p.   cm. — (A First time book) SUMMARY: Mama
Bear's reminders about the true meaning of Thanksgiving are left in the
dust as the spirit of competition takes over and Papa Bear and the cubs
begin a campaign to win first prize in the Thanksgiving Pumpkin
contest.   ISBN 0-679-80847-7 (pbk.) — ISBN 0-679-90847-1 (lib. bdg.)
[1. Thanksgiving Day—Fiction.   2. Contests—Fiction.   3. Bears—Fiction.]
I. Berenstain, Jan, 1923–   . II. Title.   III. Series: Berenstain, Stan, 1923–
First time books. PZ7.B4483Be jp 1990 [E]—dc20 90-32865 CIP AC

Manufactured in the United States of America   10 9 8 7 6 5 4 3 2 1

"Pumpkins are just like everything else in nature," said Papa Bear as he and the cubs finished weeding the pumpkin patch. "No two of them are exactly alike."

"That's for sure," agreed Brother Bear. "Look at that funny flat one and that lumpy one over there." Then there was *The Giant*, which is what Papa had named one that just seemed to be getting bigger and bigger.

"Why is it that no two things are exactly alike?" asked Sister Bear.

"It's just the way nature is," answered Papa.

"Time to wash up for supper!" called Mama Bear from the tree house steps.

"What about Queenie McBear's twin brothers?" asked Sister.

"They certainly look a lot alike," said Papa. "But I've noticed that Mrs. McBear can tell them apart quite easily."

"In you go," said Mama, shooing her family into the house.

But Sister didn't go right in.
She stood on the stoop for a
moment and looked out over
Bear Country.

It was well into fall, so the days were getting shorter. Halloween had come and gone. Pretty soon the Bears would start thinking about Christmas. But right now Bear Country was aglow in the setting sun. Farmer Ben's well-kept farm looked especially fine, with its baled hay, corn shocks, and pumpkins casting long shadows.

"I guess nature's pretty amazing," Sister said as she looked out over the beautiful scene.

"It's the most amazing thing there is," said Mama. "Come on now, in you go."

"Farmer Ben's farm sure looks beautiful in the setting sun," said Sister as the family sat down to supper.

"Humph!" said Papa grumpily. "Farmer Ben's not such a much."

"'Not such a much'?" said Mama. "Why, Ben is the finest farmer in Bear Country—and besides, he's one of your best friends."

"That may be so," said Papa. "But earlier today he came by and said, 'Nice little pumpkin patch you've got there, Papa.'"

"What he said is true," said Mama. "Especially compared to his fields and fields of pumpkins."

"That may be so, too," grumped Papa. "But I didn't like the way he said it— he sort of chuckled. My patch may be small, but The Giant is big. It may be the biggest and best pumpkin in all Bear Country. What do you think about that?"

"I think you're being oversensitive," said Mama. "Come, let's clear the table so the cubs can do their homework."

Brother and Sister sighed as they spread their books out on the table.

"What's that all about?" asked Papa.

"Oh, I was just thinking—," said Brother. "With Halloween over and Christmas almost two months away, there's nothing to look forward to."

"That's right," added Sister. "Nothing except lots of homework."

"Oh, is that so?" protested Mama Bear.

"It just so happens that there's something very important to look forward to—a very special holiday called Thanksgiving. That's when we give thanks for all the wonderful..."

"Your mama's absolutely right," interrupted Papa.

He pointed to a notice in the evening paper. It said: Don't Forget This Year's Thanksgiving Festival! Entry Blanks for the Big Pumpkin Contest Available at City Hall!

"Thanksgiving's a *very* important holiday. Especially this year, because we're going to enter The Giant in the pumpkin contest and beat the pants off Farmer Ben!"

"But Papa, he's a professional," said Brother. "He's won the contest ten years in a row!"

"All the more reason to teach him a lesson. Come on, let's go out and check up on the next heavyweight pumpkin champion of Bear Country!" he said.

Now it was Mama's turn to sigh. Thanksgiving was about giving thanks—not beating the pants off Farmer Ben.

"Isn't it a beauty?" Papa said after they admired The Giant. Across the road they could see a field of Ben's pumpkins. There were lots of fine ones, but none that measured up to The Giant.

"There's homework to be done!" called Mama Bear from the house. As they left, the cubs asked Papa, "Aren't you coming in?"

"Nope," he said. "I'm going to stay out here a little while and watch The Giant grow."

And grow it did. It grew bigger, rounder, and oranger every day.

When Papa and the cubs went to City Hall to get an entry blank for the contest, they saw the place where the winning pumpkin would go on display.

"We can't lose!" said Papa. In their mind's eye they could see their pumpkin in the place of honor.

CITY HALL

1ST

WATCH THIS SPOT FOR THE PRIZE PUMPKIN

Mama tried to remind them what Thanksgiving was really about, but every time she did, Papa would interrupt. "You'll have to excuse me, my dear," he'd say. "It's time to water The Giant."

He not only watered it on a regular schedule and gave it special plant food, he also covered it with a blanket at night and tucked it in against the cold.

One afternoon, the cubs got off the school bus with something important to tell Papa, but they were stopped in their tracks by what they saw: he was *talking to The Giant*.

COME ON, OLD BUDDY! YOU CAN DO IT! SUCK UP THAT WATER, TAKE IN THAT SUNLIGHT!

Mama explained that Papa had bought a book from the swindler Raffish Ralph about how to encourage your plants to grow by talking to them.

"Well," said Brother, "I don't suppose it can do any harm..."

"It sure could harm his reputation," said Sister, "if anybody saw him talking to a pumpkin."

"Er, Papa," Brother said, "a cub at
school told me he went on a class
trip to Ben's farm and saw some pretty
big pumpkins—especially one really
big one that Ben calls *The Monster*."

"We've got to get a look at it,"
said Papa.

That evening Papa and the
cubs climbed through the
fence into Farmer Ben's
field. They saw some
good-sized pumpkins, but
none to match The Giant.
"Maybe it's behind the
barn," whispered Papa.

Suddenly a light shone
on them and they heard Ben
shout, "Prowlers in the
pumpkin field! Get me my
pitchfork!"

They got out of there so fast Papa tore his overalls climbing through the fence.

"What have you been up to?" asked Mama Bear when they got home. "Nothing much," said Papa. "Just strolling in the moonlight!"

The weekend before Thanksgiving arrived, and it was time for the big festival. The Bear family got there just in time. The pumpkin judging was about to begin! There were many fine pumpkins in the contest. But Papa was sure that none could measure up to The Giant...*until he saw The Monster!* It was at least as big and round and orange as his pumpkin—and maybe, *just maybe,* a little bigger, rounder, and oranger.

THE GIANT

1ST Prize or Bust!

JUDGE

THE GOURD
The Jones

PUMPKIN CONTEST

The Bears waited nervously while the judges studied, measured, and weighed, and then studied, measured, and weighed some more. Finally, they made their announcement: "THE FIRST-PRIZE WINNER— *AND STILL CHAMPION...*"

Of course, that meant Farmer Ben had won. It was close—it turned out that Ben's Monster was just a little bigger, rounder, and oranger than Papa's Giant. But that wasn't the worst of it. The Giant didn't even come in second. A beautiful pumpkin grown by Miz McGrizz won second prize. The Giant came in third. Papa and the cubs were crushed...crushed and very quiet as they pushed their third-prize winner home.

It wasn't until they reached the crest of a hill that overlooked Bear Country that Mama decided to have her say. "I know you're disappointed. But third prize is nothing to be ashamed of. Besides, Thanksgiving isn't about contests and prizes. It's about giving thanks. And it seems to me that we have a lot to be thankful for."

Perhaps it was Mama's lecture, or maybe it was how beautiful Bear Country looked in the sunset's rosy glow. But whatever the reason, Papa and the cubs began to understand what Mama was talking about.

Even more so on Thanksgiving Day. After the Bears gave thanks for the wonderful meal they were about to enjoy, Sister Bear gave her own special thanks. "I'm thankful," she said, "that we *didn't* win first prize: if we had, The Giant would be on display in front of City Hall instead of being part of the yummy pies we're going to have for dessert!"

As the laughter faded and the Bears thought about the blessings of family, home, friends, and neighbors, they knew deep in their hearts that there was no question about it—indeed they did have a great deal to be thankful for.